KATHRYN DENNIS

SNAKES ON A TRAIN

Feiwel and Friends
New York

A Feiwel and Friends Book
An imprint of Macmillan Publishing Group, LLC
175 Fifth Avenue, New York, NY 10010

 Printed in China by RR Donnelley Asia Printing Solutions Ltd., Dongguan City, Guangdong Province.

Our books may be purchased in bulk for promotional, educational, or business use. Please contact your local bookseller or the Macmillan Corporate and Premium Sales Department at (800) 221-7945 ext. 5442 or by e-mail at MacmillanSpecialMarkets@macmillan.com.

Library of Congress Cataloging-in-Publication Data is available.
ISBN 978-1-250-30440-7

Book design by Rebecca Syracuse
Feiwel and Friends logo designed by Filomena Tuosto
First edition, 2019

The artwork in this book was created digitally.

1 3 5 7 9 10 8 6 4 2

mackids.com

For my brother, who always
loved snakes and trains

The conductor takes the tickets

as the snakes all slither on.

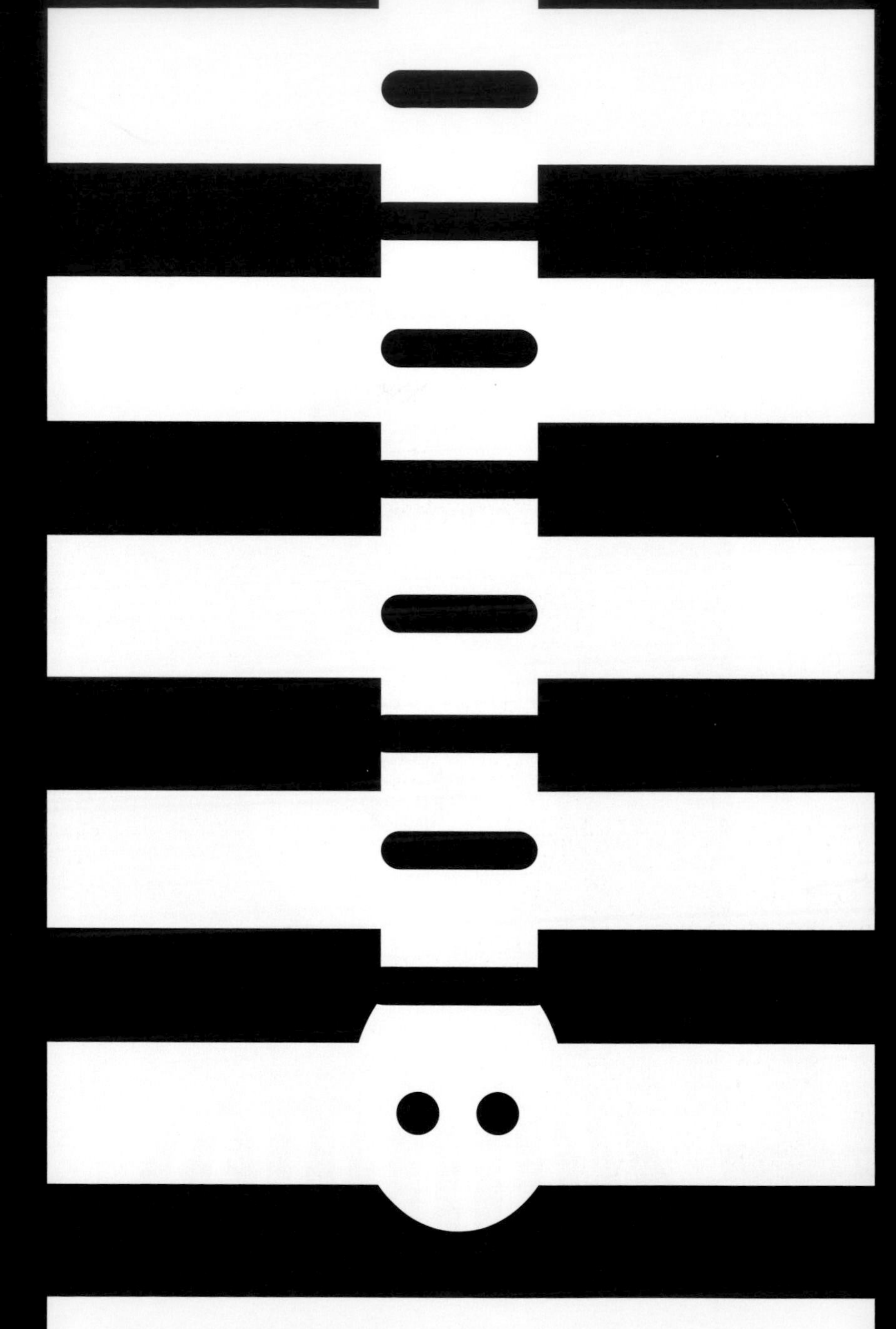

The tracks are checked.

The whistle blows. It's time to move along.
Hissssssssssssssss goes the sound of the train.

The train leaves the station
as the gears begin to grind.

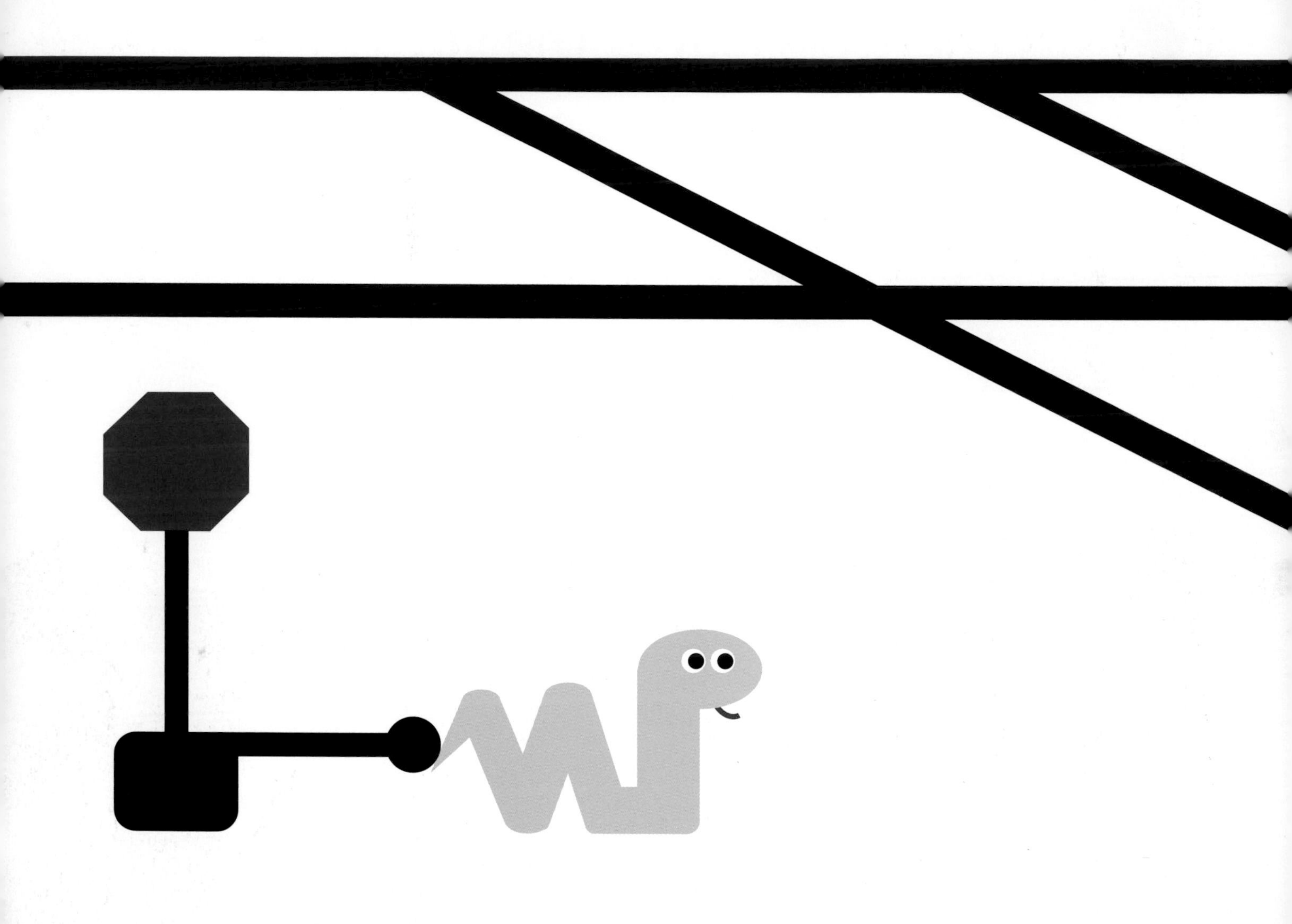

The switcher pulls the handle,
and the cars slide down the line.

Hissssssssssssssss goes
the sound of the train.

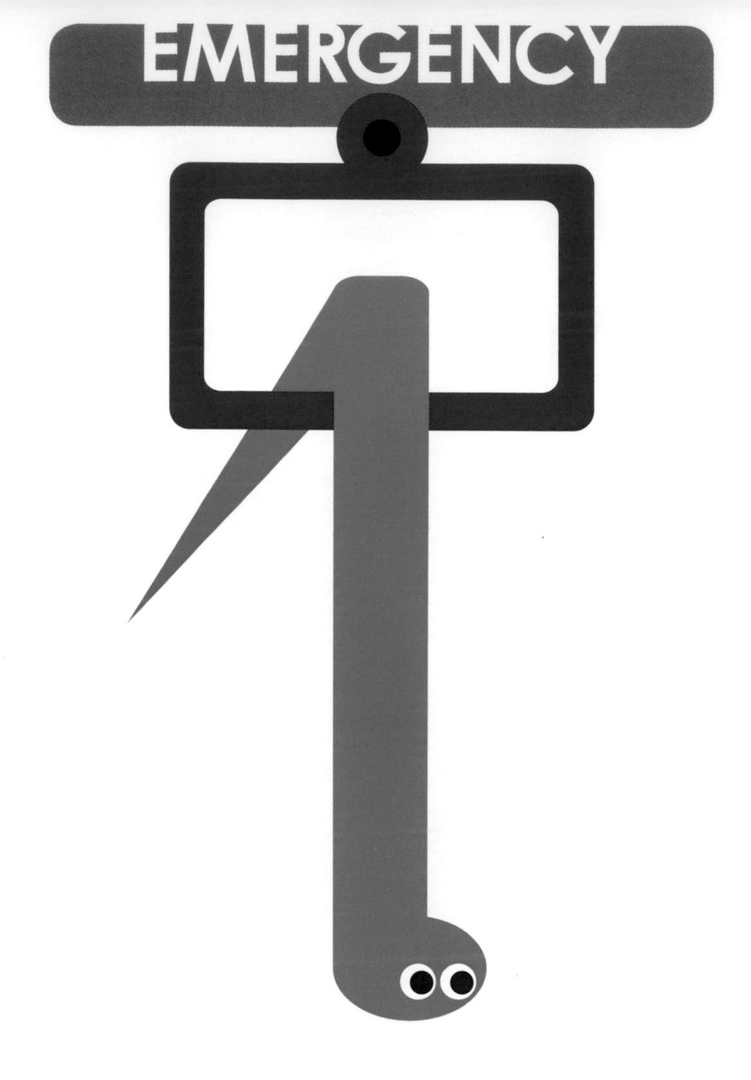

The brakesnake stops the train.

There's trouble in the back.

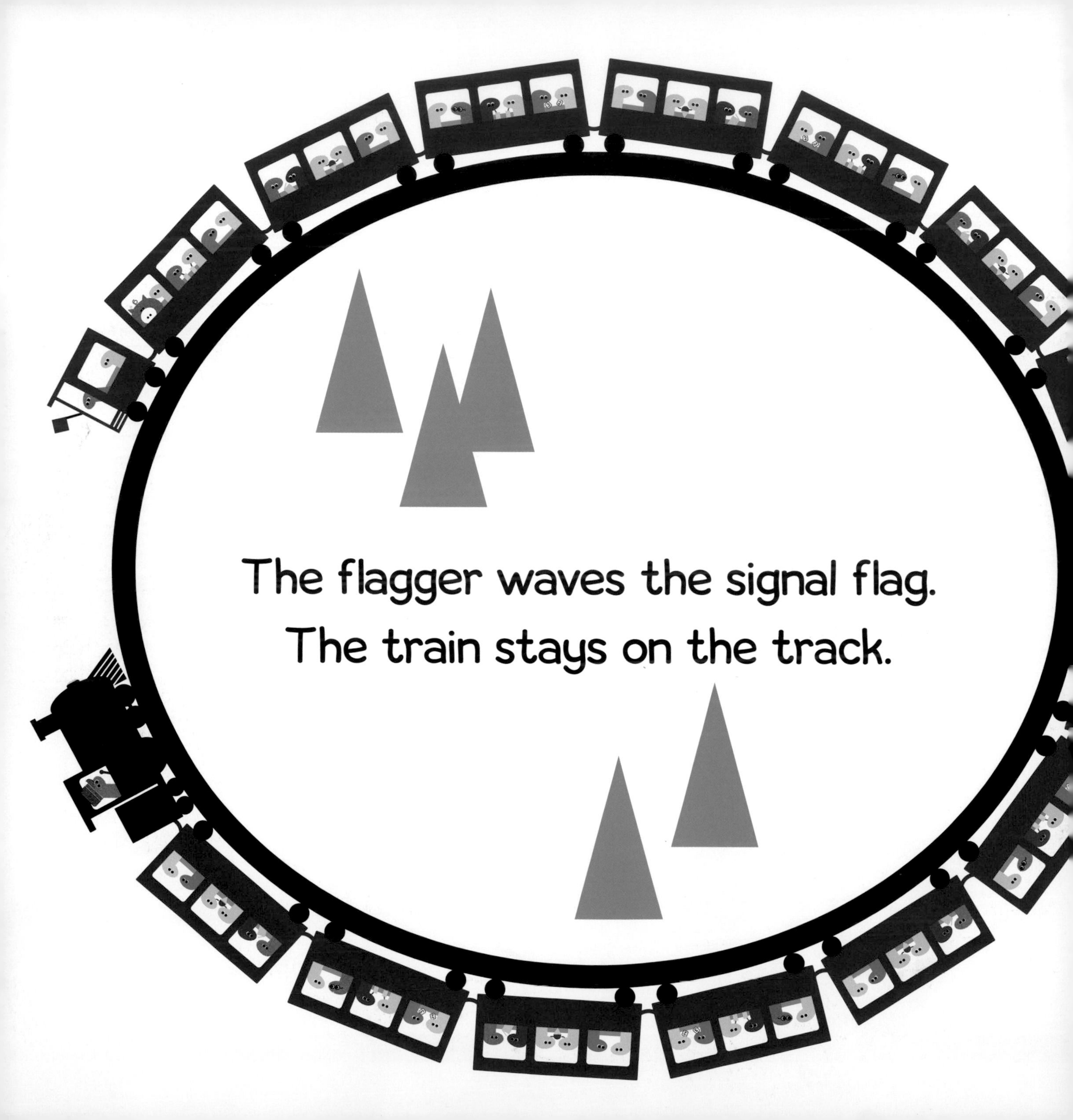

The flagger waves the signal flag.
The train stays on the track.

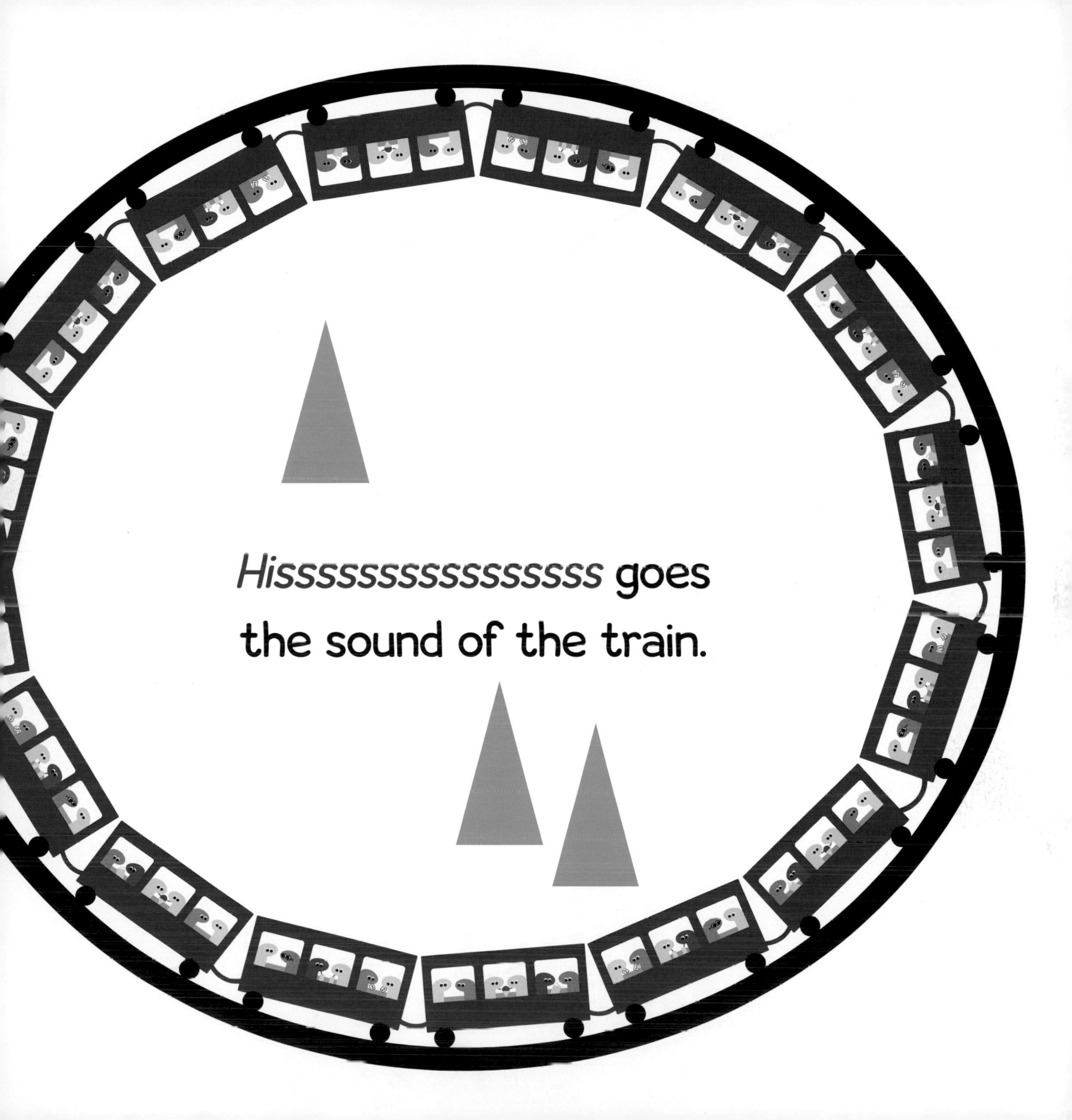

Hissssssssssssssss goes the sound of the train.

Hissssssssssssssss goes the sound of the train.

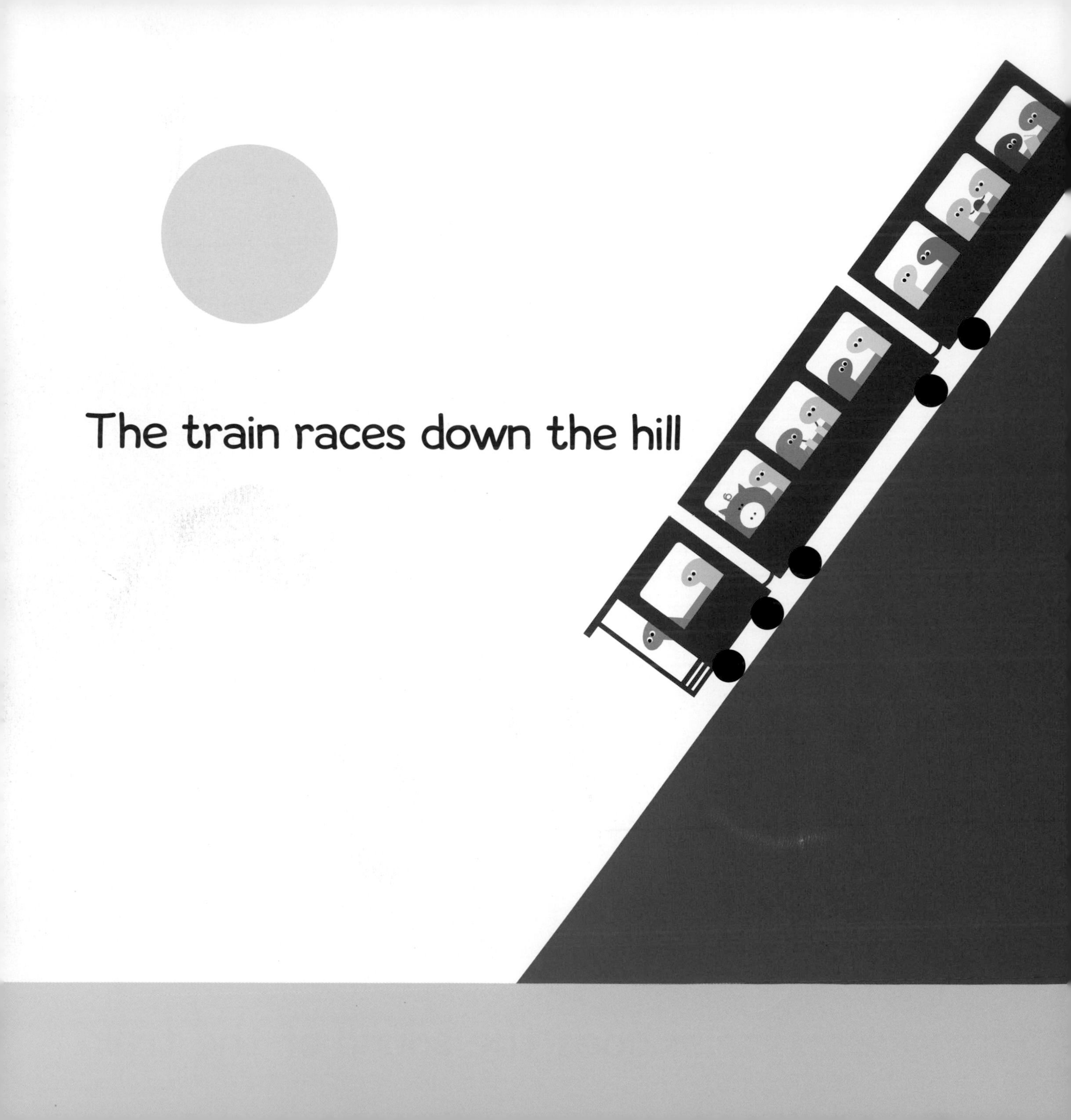

The train races down the hill

as the snakes pretend to fly.

A view from high
as fish swim by.

Hissssssssssssssss goes
the sound of the train.

The day is coming to an end.

It's time for snakes to find their dens.

As snakes slither off to sleep,

the train rests for the night.

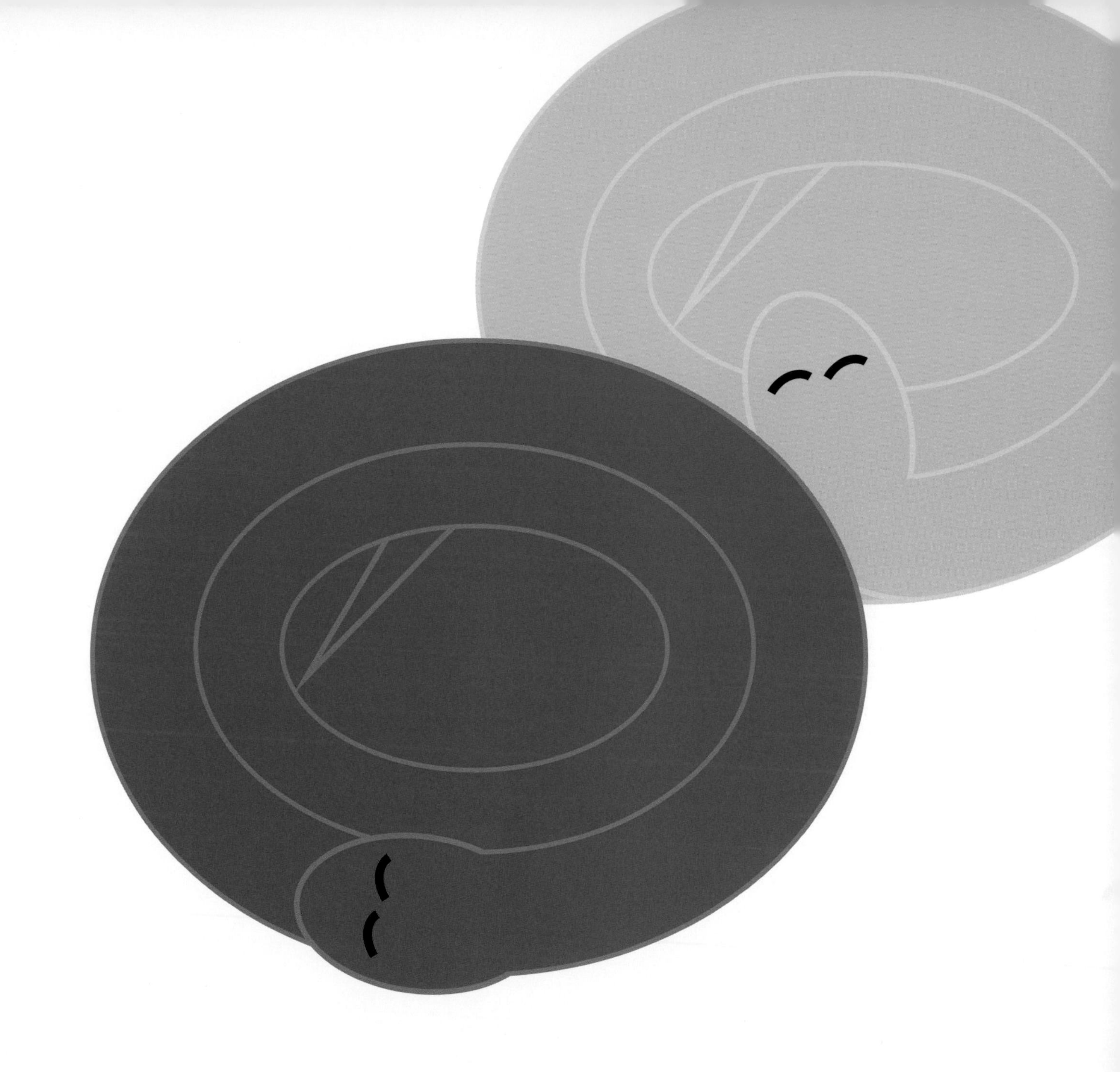

Snakes wrap themselves in little balls

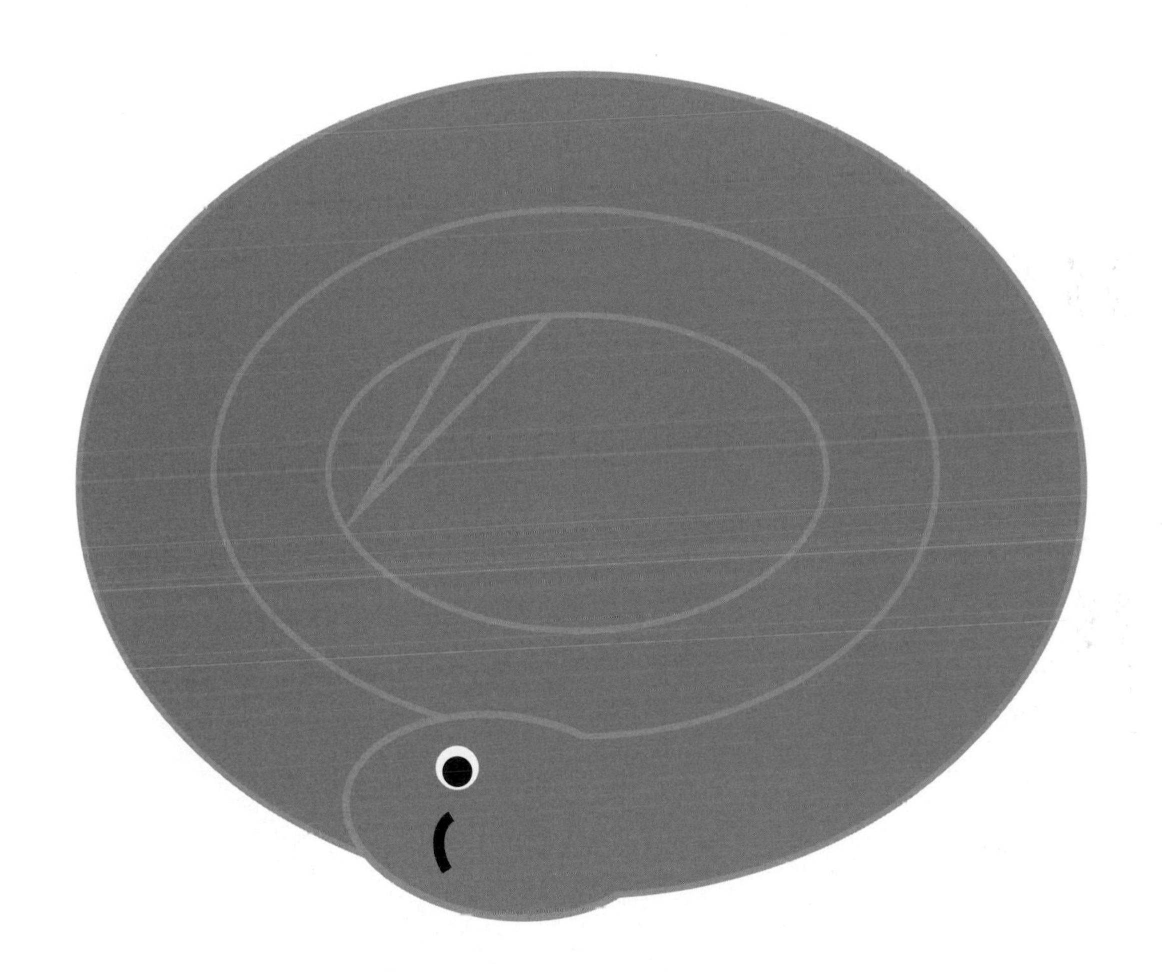

and tuck their tails in tight.

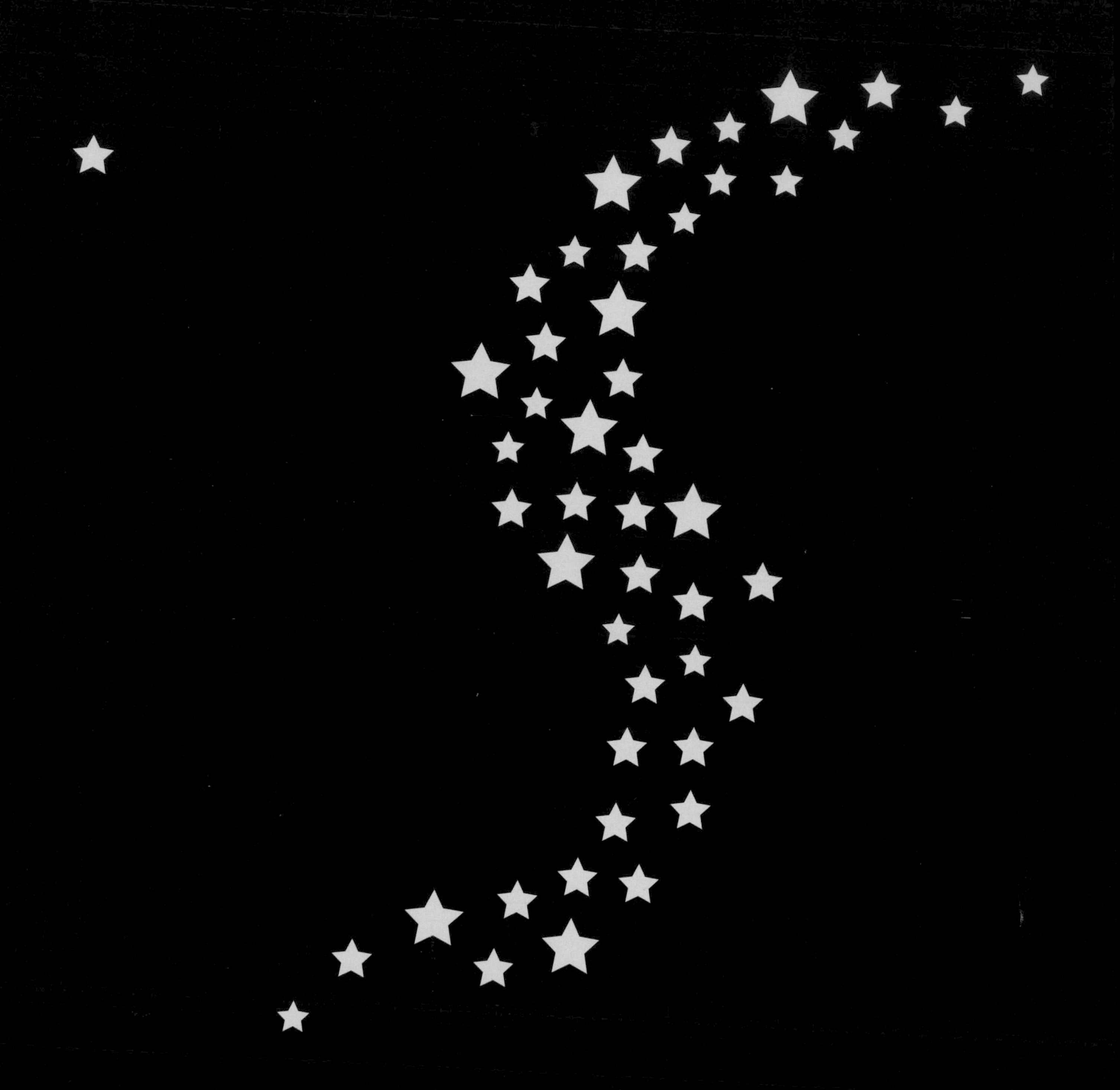

Sssssssssssssssssh goes the sound of the train.